DARTH VADER™

THE MAN, THE WARRIOR, THE COMMANDER

BENJAMIN HARPER

Brimming with creative inspiration, how-to projects, and useful information to enrich your everyday life, Quarto Knows is a favorite destination for those pursuing their interests and passions. Visit our site and dig deeper with our books into your area of interest: Quarto Creates, Quarto Cooks, Quarto Homes, Quarto Lives, Quarto Drives, Quarto Explores, Quarto Gifts, or Quarto Kids.

Inspiring | Educating | Creating | Entertaining

First Published in 2017 by becker&mayer! books, an imprint of The Quarto Group
11120 NE 33rd Place, Suite 101
Bellevue, WA 98004
www.QuartoKnows.com

This book is part of the *Star Wars Master Models: Darth Vader* kit and is not to be sold separately.

becker&mayer! books titles are also available at discount for retail, wholesale, promotional, and bulk purchase. For details, contact the Special Sales Manager by email at specialsales@quarto.com or by mail at The Quarto Group, Attn: Special Sales Manager, 401 Second Avenue North, Suite 310, Minneapolis, MN 55401 USA.

17 18 19 20 21 5 4 3 2 1

ISBN: 978-0-7603-5504-6

Library of Congress Cataloging-in-Publication Data available upon request.

Author: Benjamin Harper
Paper Engineer: Claudio Dias
Design: Sam Dawson
Editorial: Delia Greve
Production: Tom Miller

Printed, manufactured, and assembled in China, 07/17.

MIX
Paper from responsible sources
FSC® C017606

171040

Introduction

In a galaxy fraught with sinister forces, even the most dastardly villains cowered in the shadow of the Dark Lord of the Sith known as Darth Vader. Second in command to Emperor Palpatine, Vader used the Force, intimidation, and the fear of intense punishment to extract allegiance. He was legendary for his iron will and lack of feeling for anything other than his evil master, to whom he had a profound, abiding devotion.

Vader did not set out to serve a horrific galactic dictatorship. In fact, his early dreams were far more humble. As a young boy, Darth Vader—or Anakin Skywalker, as he was named before he turned to the dark side—yearned only to become an accomplished star pilot.

Fate had a different path in store for the young boy. A chance meeting with a Jedi Knight took him from his simple life into a nightmare that would destroy his friends, his family, the worlds around him, and, ultimately, his deepest self.

Though his time as a brutal Sith Lord changed him in many ways, he never lost the last spark of that hopeful boy's idealism. His crimes were appalling, his leadership terrifying, and his relationships strained. But at the end of his life, Darth Vader ended the Emperor's grip on the galaxy, bringing balance to the Force at last.

CHAPTER

1

Becoming a Sith Lord

THE PATH THAT LED THE MAN who would become Darth Vader to the dark side was one few could have predicted. As a young slave boy named Anakin Skywalker, he was humbly raised by his mother, Shmi, on the Outer Rim desert planet of Tatooine. There, he worked for a Toydarian named Watto. In his spare time, he piloted podracers for Watto in the dangerous Mos Espa competitions.

The day a Jedi Knight walked into Watto's junk shop looking for replacement hyperdrive parts, Anakin's life changed forever. Qui-Gon Jinn, Jedi and protector of Queen Amidala, sensed Anakin's formidable Force abilities. When a test revealed that Anakin's potential to master the ways of the Force was, as Qui-Gon's Padawan, Obi-Wan Kenobi, said, "off the charts," Qui-Gon knew he had to train Anakin as a Jedi. Qui-Gon sensed Anakin was the fulfillment of a Jedi Prophecy— he was the one who would bring balance to the Force.

In a risky move, Qui-Gon made a bet with Watto: If the boy won the Boonta Eve Podrace, he would earn his freedom, and Qui-Gon would get the parts he needed for his ship. Heeding Qui-Gon's first lesson, "Feel, don't think. Trust your instincts," Anakin endured the dangerous race and came out on top. Left with no choice, Watto released Anakin from his servitude. With a heavy heart, Anakin left behind his mother and his home and made for Coruscant, the capital planet of the galaxy, to begin his Jedi training.

When Qui-Gon presented Anakin to the Jedi Council on Coruscant, however, they sensed fear and anger in him. "Clouded, this boy's future is," Master Yoda warned. Defiant, Qui-Gon declared he would take Anakin on as his Padawan learner against the Council's wishes.

During the adventures on Tatooine, Anakin had formed a strong bond with Padmé Amidala—the Queen of Naboo. With the Trade Federation taking greater control of Queen Amidala's home planet, Qui-Gon and Obi-Wan left Coruscant and traveled to Naboo, where they were to protect the Queen as she attempted to take back the reins of her government. Anakin was entrusted to their care during this dangerous mission.

On Amidala's watery world, Anakin piloted a Naboo N-1 starfighter and proved

LEFT: Qui-Gon Jinn presents Anakin Skywalker to the Jedi Council for the first time.

his abilities by single-handedly destroying the Droid Control Ship that was orbiting the planet and which controlled the Trade Federation's droid armies.

Sadly, Qui-Gon Jinn was mortally wounded in his duel with the Sith Lord Darth Maul. Anakin was placed in the care of Obi-Wan Kenobi, who had been given the title of Jedi Knight due to his valiant fighting during the Battle of Naboo. With the permission of the Jedi Council, Obi-Wan took Anakin as his Padawan learner.

The resurgence of the Sith menace brought more importance to the prophecy Qui-Gon had spoken of. The Sith, nemeses of the Jedi who exploited the dark side of the Force, had been thought extinct for a thousand years. If Anakin was, in fact, the Chosen One foreseen by Qui-Gon, his training as a Jedi was essential.

Anakin went on to train with Obi-Wan Kenobi and fight beside him in many great battles. His natural abilities in the Force led him to become one of the greatest pilots in the galaxy. Although Anakin thought of Obi-Wan as the closest thing he had ever had to a father, the Padawan's natural arrogance was an impediment to his training. Student and teacher argued. Anakin believed Obi-Wan was jealous of his powers. In his mind, he accused his master of keeping things from him in order to reap more glory for himself. The dark seed in Anakin's heart had already taken root.

Ten years passed, and Anakin was given his first solo mission as a Jedi: He was to escort Padmé Amidala, now a senator representing the planet Naboo, back to her home world and keep her safe from dark forces plotting her demise. During their time together, the two fell in love.

After a deadly battle on the planet Geonosis in which many Jedi were killed, Anakin and Padmé planned to marry, despite the consequences should they be found out. Their wedding was held in secret.

RIGHT TOP: "Are you an angel?" Padmé meets Anakin in Watto's junk shop.
RIGHT BOTTOM: Anakin and Padmé get to know each other better on Naboo.

As a Jedi-in-training, Anakin made an unlikely ally—Chancellor Palpatine, who had been the senator to Naboo during the Trade Federation's occupation of the planet. The Chancellor and Anakin often met privately, Anakin telling the Chancellor of his problems. Palpatine gave Anakin advice that usually went against what his Jedi elders commanded, fueling Anakin's many internal struggles. Who was more trustworthy: the Jedi Council or the Chancellor of the Galactic Republic? Where should he place his loyalties?

ABOVE: Anakin Skywalker pledges allegiance to the Emperor, who, in turn, bestows the name Darth Vader upon him.

When war broke out in the galaxy, Anakin did his duty in the Republic Army. He fought valiantly against the Confederacy of Independent Systems and won many victories for the Republic.

A power more sinister than war was in play, however—one not even the Jedi Council sensed. A Dark Lord of the Sith had emerged and was engineering the entire war behind the scenes, playing both sides against one another, in a bid to gain total control over the galaxy.

Anakin grew more and more troubled. A darkness was spreading within him. He felt the Jedi Council didn't trust him, and he was plagued with nightmares of his wife dying horribly. When he told the Chancellor of his fears, Palpatine told him there was only one way to save Padmé from dying—the dark side of the Force.

Overrun with conflict and in terror of losing his wife, Anakin made a disastrous decision and betrayed the Jedi Order. His nature left him susceptible to the effects of suspicion and fear. And so, when Mace Windu was battling Palpatine, who had revealed himself as the mastermind behind the galactic upheaval, Anakin worked with the Dark Lord to destroy Mace Windu. He vowed undying loyalty to Palpatine. In exchange, Palpatine would help him save Padmé.

Given the name Darth Vader, the new Sith apprentice took to his identity aggressively. His first mission was to go to the Jedi Temple and eliminate all Jedi—including the Younglings—within its walls. After that, it was to Mustafar for still more killing, this time bringing an end to the war—with his own savagery.

On Mustafar, a pregnant Padmé located and confronted Anakin, who accused her of allying herself with the Jedi—now his sworn enemies. She begged him to run away with her before it was too late, but in his anger, Anakin used the Force to choke her into unconsciousness. His distrust had grown, warping his mind, destroying the parts of his character that had once suggested his potential. His reason, his humanity, his hope—Palpatine had undermined them all, contorting them the way relentless winds make trees grow crooked.

And then, in a testament to the enormity of the change he had undergone, Anakin pulled his lightsaber on his mentor. On the searing rivers of Mustafar, Anakin and Obi-Wan battled, each pulling on opposite sides of the Force. When Obi-Wan finally gained the high ground and told Anakin to concede, Anakin gave one final push and leapt through the air, forcing Obi-Wan to strike. The blow severed both of Anakin's legs, leaving him helpless on the bank of the lava river. Obi-Wan, too crushed—and too honorable—to end his old friend's life himself, told Anakin that he loved him and walked away, assuming his former Padawan would be dead in moments. Anakin, locked in his rage, had only these words for his former master: "I hate you!"

Charred and near death, Anakin was trying to drag himself up from the lava when Palpatine—newly declared as the Emperor of the Galactic Empire—came to his rescue. The Emperor took him to a secret Sith medical facility where Anakin was placed in a permanent suit of life-sustaining armor and given artificial limbs. His suit breathed for him, in a ghastly approximation of his formal, natural existence.

To fuel Darth Vader's anger further, to cement his new identity as a servant of the darkness, Palpatine lied to his apprentice, telling Vader that he himself had killed Padmé with his own hands.

With nothing left to lose or live for, Darth Vader gave himself wholly to the dark side of the Force and his new master, Emperor Palpatine.

RIGHT: Darth Vader, Sith Lord, on Mustafar.

Darth Vader's Powers

Anakin Skywalker was an incredibly powerful Jedi—one of the most powerful in the galaxy. When he turned to the dark side, he gave into anger and hatred, which allowed his powers to grow.

As a Force-user, Darth Vader was able to read and manipulate the thoughts and emotions of others, levitate objects of almost any size, leap great distances, and use the Force to choke others.

Unlike other Sith Lords, Darth Vader was unable to produce deadly Force Lightning, as both of his hands were prosthetic.

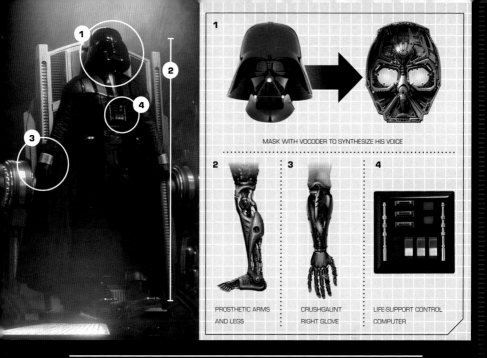

MASK WITH VOCODER TO SYNTHESIZE HIS VOICE

PROSTHETIC ARMS AND LEGS

CRUSHGAUNT RIGHT GLOVE

LIFE-SUPPORT CONTROL COMPUTER

Darth Vader's Suit

After Anakin Skywalker was defeated on Mustafar, he was left in an extremely precarious physical state. Emperor Palpatine brought the finest medical equipment and procedures, not to mention Sith alchemy, to bear in order to save his new apprentice's life. The result was a complex and intimidating life-support suit that not only maintained Darth Vader's vital systems, but also boosted his natural strength and abilities through cyborg implants. The suit was temperature-controlled, as well as fire- and blast-proof. It could even repair itself.

The entire suit had an airtight seal, ensuring optimum performance and health at all times. It was a truly diabolical creation.

1. Angled shape help protects head and neck without hindering movement
   - Imbedded vocoder synthesizes his voice
   - Optical filters display environmental data in the vision field
   - Audio sensors enhance soundwave transmission
2. Prosthetic arms and legs
3. Crushgaunt right glove
4. Life-support control computer

2 | Father, Son, and Friend

THE RELATIONSHIPS ANAKIN FORGED throughout his life—with his mother, his mentors, his wife, and, after he had become Darth Vader, his children—were troubled, chaotic, and painful. His inability to control his emotions and his greed as he navigated these complicated relationships contributed much to his fall to the dark side.

Anakin grew up in a hovel with his mother, Shmi, on Tatooine. When Qui-Gon Jinn discovered him and realized his potential to fulfill the Jedi prophecy, he had to say goodbye to Shmi, the only love and support he had ever known. This might have caused the second crack in his psyche, after the humiliation of being a slave. Leaving his mother behind filled Anakin with guilt and inspired terrible nightmares about her safety. Many years later, when he could no longer take the uncertainty, Anakin returned to Tatooine in search of his mother. He found her in the desert, having been kidnapped by Tusken Raiders. She had been tortured and was tied up, near death. He told her that he had come to take her home. Shmi told Anakin she loved him, and then she died in his arms.

Hatred rushed through Anakin's body and consumed him. He welcomed it and allowed it to take control of him. He slaughtered the Tusken Raiders, men, women, and children, in the camp before leaving with Shmi's body. He then buried her and apologized to her for not being strong enough to save her. The anguish he had felt since childhood only became greater.

Those feelings of failing his mother, of being unable to protect her, were amplified when he became a husband. When Anakin first saw Padmé Amidala, Queen of Naboo, his first words to her were, "Are you an angel?" The two soon formed a bond that lasted throughout the Battle of Naboo, until Anakin was chosen to be Obi-Wan Kenobi's Padawan.

After Anakin left Padmé and Naboo behind, he never stopped thinking of her. When an assassination attempt was made on her life, Anakin and Obi-Wan Kenobi were assigned by Chancellor Palpatine to protect Padmé from further attacks.

Outwardly, Padmé was put off by Anakin's obvious attraction to her and she rebuffed him, reminding him that a Jedi and a senator could not possibly have a

LEFT: Darth Vader fights his son, Luke Skywalker, on Cloud City.

relationship. Even after she admitted her feelings for him, she was adamant they could never be together.

Yet when they were captured on Geonosis and facing death, Padmé could no longer lie about her feelings for Anakin: She "truly, deeply" loved him. When it seemed all hope was lost, Yoda arrived with the newly formed Army of the Republic and many Jedi. The Clone Wars erupted with this first battle, and, although many Jedi were killed, the Republic—it seemed—was victorious. As though he had himself brought on bloodshed and death, even Anakin's happiness was stained.

With an urgency brought on by the onset of war, Anakin and Padmé married in a secret ceremony, before Anakin was called away to fight. They vowed to keep their marriage hidden from everyone. When Padmé told Anakin she was

ABOVE: Padmé tells Anakin she loves him as they enter the arena on Geonosis.

pregnant, after the Battle of Coruscant, they realized they wouldn't be able to keep their marriage secret any longer, and he would be expelled from the Jedi Order. It was as though a curse clung to him and he had no right to the future for which others could hope.

Anakin soon began having more nightmares, now about Padmé dying in childbirth. Anakin believed his dreams were premonitions, and he vowed to do whatever it took to keep these dreams from coming true.

Acting on impulse, Anakin threw away his entire life to do what he thought was best for Padmé. Chancellor Palpatine, now revealed as a Sith Lord, promised he could stop Padmé from dying and help Anakin protect her if only he became his apprentice. Tortured by the thought of losing his wife, overtaken by possessiveness, he fell to the dark side and under the evil bidding of his new Master. When Padmé begged him to come back to her, Anakin was blinded by the dark side of the Force and choked her into unconsciousness. Again, his feelings—even of love and selflessness—were distorted by darkness and greed.

However, it was not only Anakin's desire for love and happiness that became twisted: His drive to distinguish himself as a pilot and Jedi Knight consumed him. Qui-Gon was the first to notice Anakin's impressive Force abilities, the first to think him special. Determined to train Anakin as a Jedi, Qui-Gon freed Anakin from slavery, taking him from the Outer Rim to the center of the galaxy. Qui-Gon was Anakin's first mentor, and although his time with Anakin was brief, his impact on the boy's future was great. Sadly, Qui-Gon was killed by the Sith Lord Darth Maul, and Anakin was then entrusted by the Jedi Council into the care of Obi-Wan Kenobi, even against Master Yoda's better judgment. But it had been Qui-Gon's dying wish.

After Qui-Gon's untimely demise, Anakin trained with Obi-Wan for years to become a Jedi Knight, looking to the older Jedi as a beloved father figure. It was during this period of training that Anakin's desire to stand out, to be special among all Jedi, took root.

As Anakin's powers grew stronger, he felt trapped by the rules of the Jedi, believing he was ready to face the trials standing in the way of his becoming a Jedi Knight. He sometimes felt that Obi-Wan was jealous of his natural abilities and was holding him back. Although his rational mind railed against these dark suspicions, Anakin struggled with his anxieties.

When Anakin turned at last to the dark side of the Force, he accused Obi-Wan of turning Padmé against him. Obi-Wan pointed out that Anakin's poor choices and inability to control his emotions had been the cause of his own downfall,

ABOVE and RIGHT: Master and apprentice meet in battle once again aboard the Death Star.

but Anakin gave Obi-Wan an ultimatum: "If you're not with me, then you're my enemy."

It was a challenge that caused the former Master and apprentice to cross lightsabers. Anakin's ego and distrust of those close to him served only to fan the fire of his hatred. After Obi-Wan left Anakin broken on Mustafar, he went into seclusion on the planet Tatooine. For years, he watched over Anakin's son, Luke, whom he had placed in the care of Anakin's stepbrother, Owen, and Owen's wife, Beru.

Obi-Wan eventually resurfaced, and faced his former apprentice once again aboard the dreaded Death Star. Obi-Wan told him, "If you strike me down, I shall become more powerful than you can possibly imagine." He lowered his lightsaber, closed his eyes, and allowed Vader to kill him. It was an act of sacrifice incomprehensible to the man who was once Anakin Skywalker. It was also an act that would foreshadow Darth Vader's demise when he ultimately accepted his role as a father.

Darth Vader assumed his children had died with Padmé. He was unaware she had given birth to twins in a remote station on Polis Massa before she had given up and expired with a broken heart. His children, Luke and Leia, were spirited away and kept in secret—Yoda warned that Vader could use them to gain even more power in the galaxy, should he ever learn of their existence.

Luke was raised on Tatooine as a moisture farmer, but he dreamed of being a pilot, much like the father he had never known. In another echo of his father's childhood, Luke's path changed the day a Jedi entered his life and offered to show him a wider world.

Luke gave himself fully to the cause of the Rebel Alliance and piloted an X-wing in the Battle of Yavin. He was responsible for blowing up the first Death Star, becoming a rebel hero. Darth Vader became obsessed with tracking down the young rebel commander, only to realize that Skywalker was, in fact, his living son. When the Emperor ordered Vader to kill Luke, Vader suggested he could turn Luke as he had been. "He will join us or die," Vader said before setting off to trap his son.

Luke and Vader met face-to-face for the first time on Cloud City. Fresh off his training with Yoda on Dagobah, Luke's cockiness got the best of him. Darth Vader cornered him on a small gantry jutting out over a deep reactor shaft. Darth Vader had cut off his son's hand in battle, and, as Luke struggled to hold on, Vader extolled the virtues of the dark side.

"I'll never join you," Luke hissed in response.

"If only you knew the power of the dark side," Vader replied. "Obi-Wan never told you what happened to your father."

"He told me enough! He told me you killed him," Luke responded.

"No. I am your father," Darth Vader said. "Join me, and we can rule the galaxy as father and son."

Rather than surrender to Vader's twisted vision of the future, Luke dropped from the gantry and away from his father.

Vader did not give up his pursuit of Luke, however. The two finally met again on the forest moon of Endor when Luke surrendered to protect his friends, who had landed on the moon as part of a covert mission to destroy the shield generator protecting the second Death Star. Again, it was an act of sacrifice beyond Vader's understanding. A deep rift separated him from those who still lived by ideals of honor and courage.

Despite Luke's insistence that there was still good in his father, Vader denied him: "It is too late for me, son." His mind was fully in thrall to the Emperor and his plans. Or so he believed.

Leia's experience with her father was less uplifting than Luke's. Leia never knew Vader as anything but the planet-destroying tyrant he had shown himself to be. Not only was she subjected to the ministrations of an illegal Interrogator Droid in the course of Vader's attempt to dredge from her information about the secret Rebel Alliance base, but she also watched Vader casually stand by while her home planet was obliterated, and then as Han Solo was lowered into a carbon-freezing chamber after being casually tortured. To Leia, Vader was nothing more than the embodiment of evil who destroyed everything she cared about.

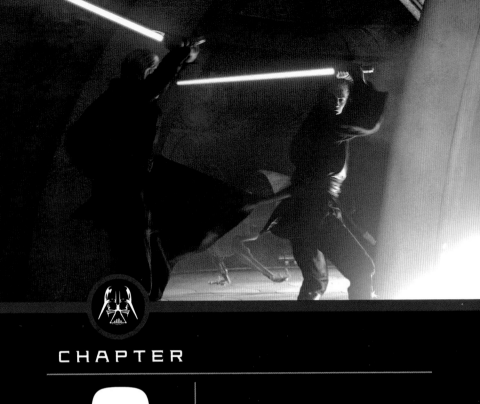

CHAPTER

3 | The Warrior

LONG BEFORE HE TURNED TO THE DARK SIDE of the Force, Anakin was known for his prowess as a pilot and as a fighter. His skills served him well during his time as a Jedi. They served him equally well after he joined the Sith and became Darth Vader. His physical abilities were only one aspect of his prowess in a fight. Mental manipulation and his powerful emotions often set him apart. The heat of a battle brought forth his darker tendencies.

The Merciless Warrior

Though embarrassed by his lack of control during the Battle of Geonosis, in which he disregarded commands from Obi-Wan Kenobi and raced headlong to fight Count Dooku, Anakin had the opportunity to settle the score against Dooku on a mission to rescue Chancellor Palpatine.

The Chancellor had been kidnapped by Separatist leader General Grievous and was being held aboard Grievous's ship, *Invisible Hand*. Obi-Wan and Anakin first had to pilot their way through an intense battle taking place above the planet Coruscant. Separatist and Republic fighters and battleships were so thick in the space above the capital planet that Anakin and Obi-Wan had to weave past them, blasting enemy ships at every turn.

They finally managed to make it onto the bridge of Grievous's ship and, with the help of R2-D2, locate the Chancellor, Count Dooku, waiting for them.

Anakin conceded to Obi-Wan's authority and said he would wait for his Master's orders, in order to avoid a repeat of their last meeting, but Count Dooku quickly dispatched the older Jedi by using his Force powers to incapacitate him.

With his Master out of the action, Anakin had to fight on his own, and he quickly bested Dooku, who fell to his knees in front of Anakin and the Chancellor. With two ignited sabers at the Sith Lord's neck, Anakin hesitated when the Chancellor ordered him to kill Dooku, stating emphatically that he needed to stand trial for his crimes. But when the Chancellor ordered him again to kill the Sith Lord, Anakin relented, giving in to his basest desires, cutting Dooku's head off. Instantly remorseful, the vestiges of his honor haunted him. Anakin said, "It isn't the Jedi way."

LEFT: Anakin Skywalker battles Count Dooku, Sith Lord Darth Tyranus, on the planet Geonosis.

The Confident Warrior

Anakin's abilities as a pilot were matched only by his skills with the lightsaber.

His superior training was obvious the first time he and Obi-Wan clashed on

Mustafar. They met each other blow-for-blow in a battle that could have

lasted forever had Anakin's arrogance and overconfidence not spurred him to

make a strategic error. After battling from the landing platform of a mining

complex, through the Separatists' boardroom and across service ducts and

collector arms, all the while dueling inches above deadly lava. Whether he

was blinded by hatred or by the belief that Obi-Wan could never best him,

Anakin leapt, placing himself in a compromised position. It was a move that

would wipe out the last vestiges of Anakin Skywalker and cement his position

as Darth Vader.

ABOVE: Darth Vader battles his former Master on the molten planet Mustafar.
ABOVE RIGHT: Darth Vader asks Luke Skywalker to rule the galaxy with him as father and son.

The Manipulative Warrior

A fight is never simply a clash of weapons. Verbal barbs can be just as effective. In Vader's first face-to-face clash with Luke Skywalker, he showed himself adept at mental manipulation. After luring Luke to Cloud City, Darth Vader found the young Jedi wielding a lightsaber. Vader's goal was to deliver Skywalker to the Emperor alive. Using the Force more than his lightsaber, Vader began by teasing him about his training and his relationship with Obi-Wan. As Luke battled, the Sith Lord next unleashed a hail of objects, finally breaking a vacuum-sealed window. Luke was sucked out of the reactor room. Next, Darth Vader unleashed a terrible truth in the hopes of shattering Luke's will and pushing him into the arms of the Emperor. Luke proved resistant to the manipulation and decided it would be better to fall into the unknown than follow in his father's footsteps.

Darth Vader's Lightsaber

As a Jedi, Anakin had constructed his own lightsabers, and as a Sith Lord, he had to undertake the task once again. Sith lightsabers, unlike those fashioned by the Jedi, were powered by synthetic crystals that gave them their red beams. Vader modeled his new Sith lightsaber after his previous one, but he placed a black emitter shroud at the blade's ignition point, as opposed to the original's silver shroud.

⊢ Blade Emitter

⊢ Activation Stud

⊢ Hand Grip

TIE Advanced X1

While standard TIE fighters were crude, inexpensive ships, Darth Vader's personal fighter, the TIE Advanced X1, was one of a kind. Not only did it feature life-support, it also was capable of jumps to light speed. Its targeting computer was more advanced than those of standard TIE fighters, and its unique bent wings gave it increased speed and maneuverability. Unlike its predecessors, the TIE Advanced X1 also had protective shields.

4 | The Commander

DARTH VADER FOLLOWED ONE RULE: The Emperor was always right. Although Vader was Emperor Palpatine's trusted apprentice, he was not officially—at least at first—the Emperor's second in command. Though loyal to the Emperor and willing to do his Master's bidding, Vader also bent to the command of Grand Moff Tarkin. Once Tarkin was destroyed, along with the first Death Star, Vader's place in the Imperial echelon was solidified and no Imperial officer dared question him.

Darth Vader ruled through abject terror. By making sure his underlings in the Imperial fleet were too petrified to disappoint, Darth Vader always got his way and got things done. Officers quaked in fear as Vader barked orders, doing whatever it took to please him.

The End of the Jedi Order

When the Emperor declared total control over the galaxy, his first order to Vader was simple: Destroy all Jedi. They were the enemy, he claimed. They had instigated the war as a means to take over the Galactic Senate. Darth Vader took on his task with no hesitation. If he was to rule at the Emperor's side, he had to prove he was troubled by no doubt, that no qualm could blunt his power. Flanked by clone troopers, Vader stormed the Jedi Temple on Coruscant and did not leave until every last Jedi within its hallowed walls was dead. He then led the search across the galaxy to ensure that the once-great Jedi Order and every known Force-user had been destroyed.

Death Star plans and the Battle of Yavin

Later, the Emperor charged Darth Vader with finding the rebels who had stolen technical readouts for the Death Star. In this mission, Vader followed his customary merciless style, leaving a trail of destruction and slaughtered soldiers in his wake.

After he discovered an escape pod had been jettisoned during a brief skirmish with the *Tantive IV*, he sent troops to retrieve any information it may have been carrying. The troops discovered the pod had contained only droids, which had been taken by a clan of Jawa traders. Under Vader's command, the stormtroop-

LEFT: Darth Vader and his troops set a trap for Luke Skywalker on Cloud City.

ers tracked down the Jawas and eliminated them. When the search for the droids led to Luke's aunt and uncle, they were killed for standing in the way of Vader's search.

When the droids, along with Obi-Wan Kenobi, Luke, and Leia, managed to find their way onto the Death Star, Vader sensed Kenobi's presence on the battle station and alerted Grand Moff Tarkin to that disturbance in the Force. Tarkin dismissed the warning, but as he did, he received word of a breech in the detention block where Princess Leia was being held.

Darth Vader took control of the situation and faced Obi-Wan Kenobi alone. Although Luke and Leia used Darth Vader's battle with Obi-Wan to make their escape, they were unaware that Darth Vader had cunningly placed a tracking device aboard the *Millennium Falcon* in order to discover the location of the Rebel Alliance base.

Although Grand Moff Tarkin was nervous about allowing them to escape, he trusted Darth Vader's plan and, in turn, discovered the rebels hiding on a moon called Yavin 4.

When it turned out the rebels had in fact gained access to the Death Star's plans and found a weakness in the space station, Darth Vader again took charge of the matter. In his TIE Advanced XI, flanked by two TIE fighters, Vader joined the dogfight surrounding the battle station. Vader shot down several rebel pilots singlehandedly. When the enemy had been reduced to just one lone X-wing starfighter, Darth Vader zeroed in on Luke as he was careening through the equatorial trench of the Death Star toward the exhaust port into which he would launch a proton torpedo. Whether it was Vader's position or his arrogance, he did not see the *Millennium Falcon* appear just as his targeting computer finally

LEFT TOP: Darth Vader adjusts his targeting computer during the Battle of Yavin.
LEFT BOTTOM: A surprise attack sends Darth Vader's TIE Advanced X-1 spiraling out of control.

locked on Luke. Just as Vader pulled the trigger, a blast from behind hit one of his wingmen, who crashed into Darth Vader's fighter, sending him spiraling away from the Death Star. As he regained control of his fighter, he soared away from the space station just as it exploded. Reeling from this defeat, Vader had a new purpose: to find and destroy the rebels responsible for destroying the Death Star.

Hoth Ground Assault

Aboard the Super Star Destroyer *Executor*, Vader oversaw his obsessive task by sending probe droids throughout the galaxy. Their mission was to search for signs of a new Rebel Alliance base. When one sent back images from the planet Hoth, Darth Vader knew immediately that the rebels were hiding on the distant, icy world.

He commanded Admiral Ozzel to prepare the fleet to attack Hoth, and General Veers to ready his troops. When the Imperial fleet came out of light speed, they detected an energy shield protecting the icy world, making it impossible for the Empire to attack from space. Darth Vader ordered a surface attack. Once the AT-ATs had destroyed the generator creating and maintaining the energy shield, Vader flew down to the rebel base in search of Luke Skywalker, only to watch the *Millennium Falcon* blast its way out of the landing bay.

The base lay in ruins, but Vader was not satisfied. An ion cannon had allowed most of the rebels to travel safely past the Imperial fleet, shooting bursts of energy that temporarily shorted out the Imperial ships' systems. Vader recognized the *Millennium Falcon* as the ship that had been aboard the Death Star and demanded it be captured at any cost, even as the craft fled into a nearby asteroid field. When Admiral Piett relayed to Vader the dangers of the asteroid field and said they didn't dare follow the *Millennium Falcon* for fear of damage,

RIGHT: Darth Vader and his troops invade the Rebel Alliance's Echo Base on the ice planet Hoth.

Darth Vader coolly replied, "Asteroids do not concern me, Admiral. I want that ship, not excuses."

At his command, the battle-damaged fleet charged headlong into the asteroid belt in pursuit of the fleeing ship.

The Second Death Star

Because the construction and development of the second Death Star was sluggish, Darth Vader brought the station under his own leadership. As his shuttle landed, the commanding officer greeted him with trepidation.

"Lord Vader, this is an unexpected pleasure," the commander offered.

"You may dispense with the pleasantries, commander," Darth Vader replied. "I am here to put you back on schedule."

Vader held no sympathy for the commander's excuses. Now fully established in his role as the Emperor's enforcer, Vader let nothing trouble him except falling short of perfection. By informing the commander of the Emperor's visit, Vader used simple threats to achieve his goals. Gone were the nagging doubts, the troubling remnants of his former self. He belonged to the Emperor and his brutal Empire completely.

RIGHT TOP: Darth Vader arrives on the second Death Star to deliver some distressing news to Moff Jerjerrod.
RIGHT BOTTOM: Darth Vader greets the Emperor as he disembarks for an inspection of the second Death Star.

Darth Vader's Cold Rage

Vader's impatience with those he felt were incompetent or beneath his own skills was evident in his treatment of those under his command. Evoking Darth Vader's rage held dire consequences. When Admiral Ozzel jumped out of hyperspace too close to the Hoth system, he inadvertently alerted the rebels to the Imperial presence, giving them time to prepare an ordered defense and escape. "He felt surprise was wiser," General Veers said, half-heartedly. "He is as clumsy as he is stupid," Darth Vader replied, calling up Ozzel on the view screen. As Ozzel began to speak, he started choking and gasping for air. "You have failed me for the last time, Admiral," Darth Vader said as Ozzel sunk to the floor and died. "You are in command now, Admiral Piett," Vader said before ending the communication.

Another demonstration of Vader's cool brutality occurred when a Star Destroyer captain fell afoul of the Sith Lord. After blasting free from the gut of a space slug, the *Millennium Falcon* moved into attack position against the Destroyer. An excited Captain Needa alerted Darth Vader that they had the *Millennium Falcon* in their sights. However, after the *Falcon* blasted past the Star Destroyer's bridge, it disappeared from the ship's scopes. When a communication came in from Vader demanding an update, Captain Needa felt it best to report his failure in person, stating he would apologize and take full responsibility for losing the *Falcon*. He prepared a shuttle and boarded Darth Vader's ship.

Darth Vader's cold stare and Force manipulation brought the Captain to his knees. "Apology accepted, Captain Needa," Darth Vader said as Captain Needa fell over at his feet, dead.

Super Star Destroyer *Executor*

Darth Vader commanded his fleet from *Executor*, a massive *Super*-class Star Destroyer. At 12,800 meters long, this ship carried a massive array of starfighters, including TIE interceptors, TIE bombers, and TIE fighters. It also housed a full complement of stormtroopers and various vehicles for all-terrain ground assaults, including twenty-four AT-ATs and fifty AT-STs. Darth Vader's personal quarters aboard *Executor* included the Qabbrat, his meditation chamber (the only location in which Darth Vader could safely remove his helmet and armor, due to its high pressure and supply of sterilized hyper-oxygen).

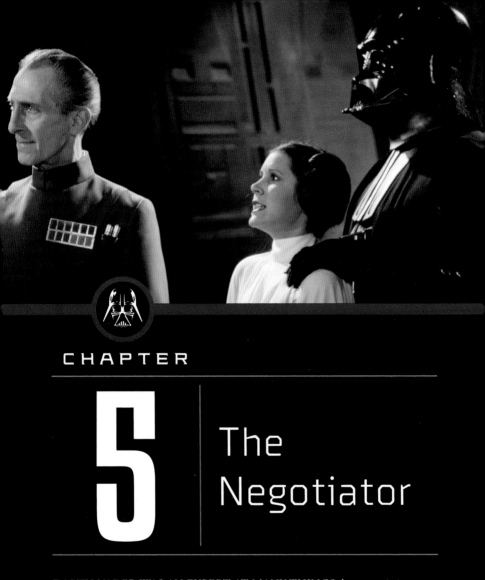

CHAPTER

5 | The Negotiator

DARTH VADER WAS AN EXPERT AT MANY THINGS, but negotiating was not one of them. Vader saw no use for it. He did not care for bargains, discussions, pleas, or any other manner of dealing that would keep him from his purpose. In fact, those who begged or debated were subject to worse punishments than those who just accepted his word. When opposed by Darth Vader, often the wisest course was instant surrender.

Peace Negotiations

When Palpatine declared himself Emperor of the First Galactic Empire at the end of the Clone Wars, Vader was assigned to meet with the remaining Separatist leaders, who had regrouped on Mustafar awaiting further instruction.

"I am sending my new apprentice, Darth Vader. He will . . . take care of you," the Emperor ominously told the anxious Separatists.

Once Vader arrived, the Separatists thought the war would finally be over, and they could discuss terms. They believed they understood their adversary. They had no idea how the Sith saw the world. Upon his arrival, Vader's attitude toward discussion was made clear when he sealed off all escape routes. "The war is over! Lord Sidious promised us peace!" Nute Gunray pleaded. There was no conversation as Vader killed the Separatists, one by one.

Diplomatic Negotiations

While Princess Leia traveled on a desperate mission to bring stolen readouts for the Death Star to the Rebel Alliance base, where the plans could be analyzed for potential weaknesses, she found herself at the mercy of a Star Destroyer. Her puny diplomatic ship, *Tantive IV,* fought against the Imperial juggernaut valiantly, but in the end her craft was defeated.

When Darth Vader boarded the Princess's craft, its designation as a diplomatic starship meant little to Vader. Protocols or any such impediment meant little to him if they stood in the way of getting what he was after. He ordered the Senator from Alderaan taken prisoner and a false distress signal sent out to report that all aboard the craft had been killed.

LEFT: Darth Vader restrains Princess Leia as she witnesses the destruction of her home planet, Alderaan.

He confronted the ship's captain, Raymus Antilles, about the stolen information, lifting the hapless rebel from the floor and, after Antilles wheezed that the ship had received no stolen transmissions, broke the man's neck.

Power Negotiations

Darth Vader's extreme "negotiation" style wasn't reserved for his enemies alone. When in a meeting aboard the Death Star, the Sith Lord did not take too kindly to Imperial General Motti's assertion that the Death Star was now the ultimate power in the universe and that the Empire should use it immediately to instill fear across the star systems.

"Don't be too proud of this technological terror you've constructed," Darth Vader cautioned. "The ability to destroy a planet is insignificant next to the power of the Force."

General Motti, in turn, mocked Darth Vader's "sad devotion to that ancient religion," noting that the Force had not assisted Darth Vader in his search for the stolen Death Star plans. Darth Vader's response was to simply raise his hand and apply a Force choke on the general. "I find your lack of faith disturbing," Darth Vader said, before releasing his victim.

Business Negotiations

After the destruction of the first Death Star, Darth Vader became obsessed with finding the rebels—in particular, Luke Skywalker.

The Battle of Hoth proved to be a failure for the Empire, as the rebels were able to escape. Darth Vader had been present for the battle and knew that the rebels had fled the icy planet in droves.

RIGHT: Darth Vader does not take kindly to General Motti's opinion of the Force.

Vader also knew that if he were able to capture Princess Leia and Han Solo, Luke Skywalker would rush to their rescue—so predictable are those burdened by a sense of compassion.

The bounty hunter Boba Fett had tracked the *Millennium Falcon* and knew it was heading for the tibanna gas colony of Cloud City, above the planet Bespin. He alerted Darth Vader, who arrived at the mining colony before the rebels to set a trap for them.

Darth Vader met with Lando Calrissian, administrator of Cloud City, and made a bargain with him: allow the Empire to use Han Solo and Princess Leia as bait to lure Luke Skywalker, and Cloud City would remain free of an Imperial presence. Realizing that if he did not cooperate the Empire would take control of the city, Lando relented, granting Darth Vader and his troops full access. Vader informed

Lando Calrissian that Princess Leia and Chewbacca were never again to leave Cloud City. When Lando balked at this change to their original terms, Vader quipped, "Perhaps you think you're being treated unfairly?" Lando, realizing his error in challenging Darth Vader, yielded. "No," he said timidly. "Good," Darth Vader replied. "It would be unfortunate if I had to leave a garrison here."

Darth Vader's plan was simple—get Luke into a carbonite freezing chamber, freeze him, and then take him to the Emperor, where they could begin the arduous process of turning Luke to the dark side.

Vader wanted to make sure the freezing process wouldn't harm Luke Skywalker, so he tested the chamber on Han Solo, after which he would give the helpless Solo to Boba Fett for transport to Jabba the Hutt.

Later, after testing the device on Han Solo, Vader ordered Princess Leia and Chewbacca taken to his ship. When Lando complained that their removal was not part of their agreement, Darth Vader snapped, "I am altering the deal. Pray I don't alter it any further," and walked away.

ABOVE: Darth Vader inspects the carbon-freezing chamber he plans to use in his trap for Luke Skywalker.
RIGHT: Darth Vader alters his deal with Lando Calrissian.

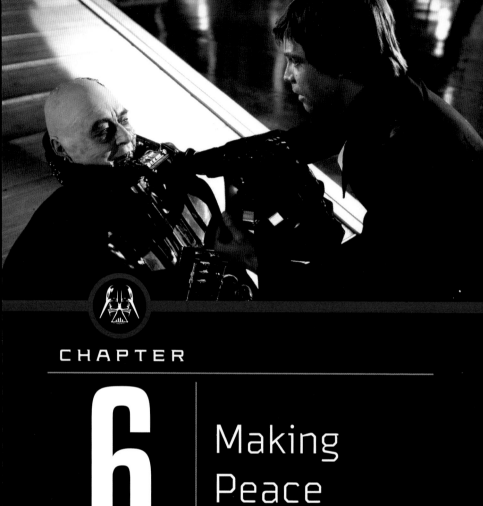

6 | Making Peace

WHEN DARTH VADER FINALLY CAPTURED HIS SON and brought him before the Emperor. The sinister Palpatine tried to convince young Skywalker to turn to the dark side and join him in ruling the galaxy, but Luke refused. Only when Palpatine informed Luke that the rebellion and all of his friends were walking into a trap—that the second Death Star was, in fact, fully operational—and that the Rebel Alliance was doomed, did Luke Skywalker take up his lightsaber to strike down the vicious dictator.

Protecting his Master, Darth Vader intervened. Father and son then engaged in an emotional battle before the Emperor's gleeful visage, Luke's anger becoming more and more apparent as the Emperor and Darth Vader taunted him mercilessly. Finally, Luke hid, realizing that he was teetering dangerously close to allowing his emotions to control him. As he tried to regain composure and reclaim his footing, Darth Vader sensed Luke's concern for his friends and for . . . his *sister*.

Vader had not known Princess Leia was Luke's twin, but it was now clear.

"So, you have a twin sister! Your feelings have now betrayed her, too. Obi-Wan was wise to hide her from me. Now his failure is complete. If you will not turn to the dark side," Darth Vader hissed, "then perhaps *she* will."

The thought of Darth Vader pursuing Leia filled Luke with a primal rage. He launched himself from his hiding place and attacked Darth Vader with his full force, overpowering the Dark Lord and leaving him weak and defeated.

The Emperor, witnessing Luke's precarious emotional state, asked the young Skywalker to fulfill his destiny and replace his father as the Emperor's second in command.

Luke refused, tossing his lightsaber away. "You've failed, your Highness," Luke replied. "I am a Jedi, like my father before me."

"So be it, *Jedi*," the Emperor grimaced. "If you will not be turned, then you will be destroyed!" And with that, he unleashed a fire of Force lightning that tore through Luke's body, ravaging it.

LEFT: Anakin Skywalker meets his son, Luke, for the first time.

Darth Vader struggled to his feet and took his place beside the Emperor as he cruelly tortured Luke with lightning.

"Father, please!" Luke screamed through the pain, hoping the man he believed was still inside Vader would hear him. Vader looked on emotionless, until finally Luke's agony pierced the armor of his dark side hatred. He lifted up the Emperor and hurled him down an open shaft and directly into the Death Star's power core.

An unnatural burst of Force energy rushed up from the chasm and filled the chamber. It ravaged the injured Darth Vader's body, causing irreparable damage to the already precarious Sith Lord. Vader gasped, his breathing apparatus failing. Luke realized the man who had once been his father had returned from the dark side.

"Luke, help me take this mask off," Anakin said. Luke warned his father that removing the mask would kill him, but Anakin knew he was already dying. "Just once, let me look on you with my own eyes," his father said.

After Luke took off his father's life-support system, Anakin told Luke to save himself.

"I've got to save you," Luke told his father. "You already have," Anakin replied. "You were right about me," Anakin whispered. "Tell your sister, you were right."

At that moment, his deepest nature was revealed again at last. Anakin became one with the light side of the Force. Luke took his father's body back with him to the forest moon of Endor. Luke set up a funeral pyre for the man whom he had known only for a moment as the great Jedi who had been his father.

Although Anakin's path had been filled with terror, struggle, and pain, his final act proved he was, indeed, the Chosen One. He had served evil, caused countless

RIGHT: Luke says goodbye to his father next to his funeral pyre on the forest moon of Endor.

deaths, created a major rift that had torn the galaxy apart, and delivered power into the clutches of the Sith. But at the end, he reached out from the darkness and climbed back into the light, bringing balance to the Force by sacrificing himself and saving his son.

ABOVE: Like the impression cast by his silhouette, Darth Vader's influence was felt across the galaxy.